156996

For
Grandad Sid.
Writer. Friend. Eejit.

PEACHTREE PUBLISHERS
1700 Chattahoochee Avenue
Atlanta, Georgia 30318-2112

www.peachtree-online.com

Text and illustrations © 2011 by Alex T. Smith

Originally published in Great Britain in 2011 by Hodder Children's Books
First United States edition published in 2013 by Peachtree Publishers

Artwork created digitally. Title is hand lettered; text is typeset in Italian Garamond BT.

Printed and bound in 2012 in China by RR Donnelley & Sons
10 9 8 7 6 5 4 3 2 1
First Edition

Library of Congress Cataloging-in-Publication Data

Smith, Alex T.
   Claude in the city / written and illustrated by Alex T. Smith.
       p. cm.
   Summary: When Claude, a small, plump dog, and his friend, Sir Bobblysock, visit the city Claude heroically, if accidentally, stops a thief, then, when Sir Bobblysock becomes ill, Claude rushes him to a hospital and is mistaken for a doctor.
   ISBN: 978-1-56145-697-0 / 1-56145-697-7
   [1. Dogs-Fiction. 2. Socks-Fiction. 3. Heroes-Fiction. 4. City and town life-Fiction. 5. Hospitals-Fiction. 6. Humorous stories.] I. Title.
   PZ7.S6422Clc 2013
   [E]-dc23
                                        2012028081

CLAUDE

in the City

ALEX T. SMITH

Ω
PEACHTREE
ATLANTA

This is Claude.

Say hello, Claude.

4

Claude is a dog.
Claude is a small dog.
Claude is a small,
plump dog.

Claude is a small, plump dog
who wears a berct and
a lovely red sweater.

Beret

Lovely sweater

Claude lives in a house with
Mr. and Mrs. Shinyshoes.

Here they are now.

Claude also lives with his best
friend, Sir Bobblysock.

Sir Bobblysock is both a sock and
quite bobbly.

He is grubby and smells a bit like
cheese.

Every morning after breakfast,
Mr. and Mrs. Shinyshoes put on their
shiny shoes and their warm coats.

Claude watches them from his bed.

He watches them with one beady
eye open and one beady eye closed,
like this:

Or sometimes like this:

"Be a good boy, Claude!"
says Mr. Shinyshoes.

"We'll be back soon!"
says Mrs. Shinyshoes.

And off they go to work.

As soon as the door has closed behind them, Claude opens both beady eyes. He takes his beret out from underneath his pillow and pops it on his head.

Then he decides what
adventure he is going
to have that day.

One morning, Claude put on his beret and decided to go to the City.

"I think I will go to the City," he said.

Sir Bobblysock came too, as he didn't have anything else planned that day.

Claude had never been to the City before. He couldn't believe how tall all the buildings were. They stretched right up into the air and some of them disappeared into the clouds.

Sir Bobblysock was glad that he wasn't the one who had to clean the windows.

The city was big and bright and very, very busy. There was so much to do!

14

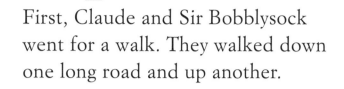

First, Claude and Sir Bobblysock
went for a walk. They walked down
one long road and up another.

Everybody seemed very friendly!

Cars beeped their horns and
some drivers shouted at them.

But it was too noisy for Claude
to hear what they were saying.
Sir Bobblysock was slightly deaf
in one ear so he was no help at all.

Next, they went to look at the pigeons. There were lots of pigeons in the city.

Claude looked at them very closely and from every angle.

He looked

⇒ secretly

⇒ shyly

⇒ and as if he was trying
not to look at them at all.

Claude decided
that he liked
pigeons
very much
indeed!

By eleven o'clock, Claude was
feeling a little bit thirsty so he went
to a fancy café with Sir Bobblysock.

Claude ordered a large hot
chocolate with marshmallows
and a straw.

Sir Bobblysock ordered a big, fruity cocktail, which looked more like a potted plant!

Claude's drink was delicious and he drank every drop. Sir Bobblysock wasn't sure where to start with his drink.

Now it was time to go shopping!

Claude was amazed that there were so many different sorts of shops.

There were
shoe shops,
loo shops,
chip shops,
and chop shops
(which were really
butcher shops).

There were even shops selling the
most curious contraptions Claude
had ever seen.

Then Sir Bobblysock discovered
the best shop in the world.

Ever.

Claude hurried inside and bought
a beret in every color and every
pattern.

Betty's Beret BOUTIQUE

That was an awful
lot of berets.

29

As they were setting off to find some lunch, Claude spotted a very interesting building.

It had lots of steps and some big pillars at the front. It was exactly the same color as juicy bones. Juicy bones happened to be Claude's favorite thing, after Sir Bobblysock and his beret.

30

RECEPTION

So Claude and Sir Bobblysock went inside. A helpful person sitting behind a big desk told them the building was an art gallery.

"Here is a guide," she said, and
handed Claude a guidebook.
"It tells you what is in each room."

Claude said thank you, left his
boxes with her, and set off with
Sir Bobblysock.

He really liked looking at things
and wanted to start straight away.

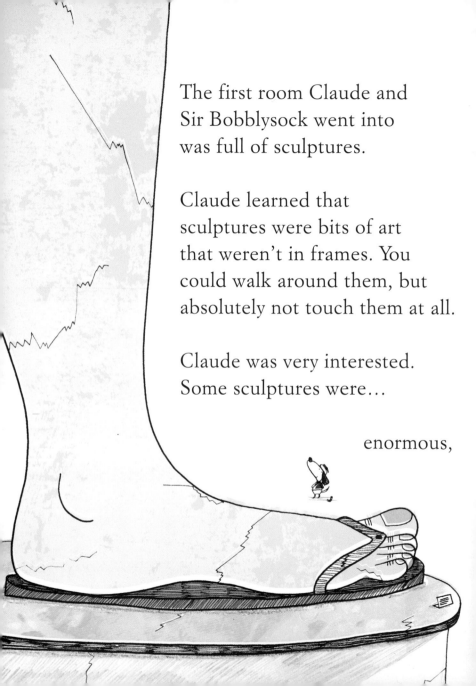

The first room Claude and
Sir Bobblysock went into
was full of sculptures.

Claude learned that
sculptures were bits of art
that weren't in frames. You
could walk around them, but
absolutely not touch them at all.

Claude was very interested.
Some sculptures were…

enormous,

 some were tiny,

and some were
very rude indeed.

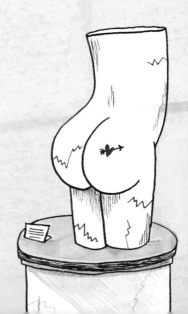

35

Claude looked at
his guidebook.

It said "Go into
the next room."

So he did.

36

On the walls were lots of
pictures in swirly frames.

Claude and Sir Bobblysock
sat down on a handy bench
and looked at them.

Some of the
paintings showed
people standing
around and pointing
at things that
weren't there.
Claude thought this
was a little bit silly.

Some of the paintings
had dogs in them,
which made Claude
happy.

"Let's go and have some lunch,"
said Claude to Sir Bobblysock.
"I could eat a juicy bone baguette!"

Claude collected his boxes
of berets and they set
off to find a café.

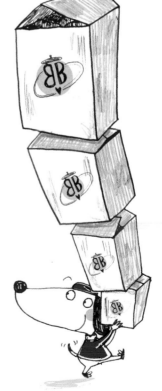

Suddenly, a naughty thief ran past
them, carrying one of the sculptures.

Two guards ran after her.

Claude's paws were so full of boxes
and his brain so full of
juicy bone baguette
that he did not
see the thief.

40

The thief did not see Claude and all
his boxes...

BUMP!

CRASH!

WALLOP!

Berets exploded everywhere.

The thief fell to the ground.

The sculpture flew through the air.

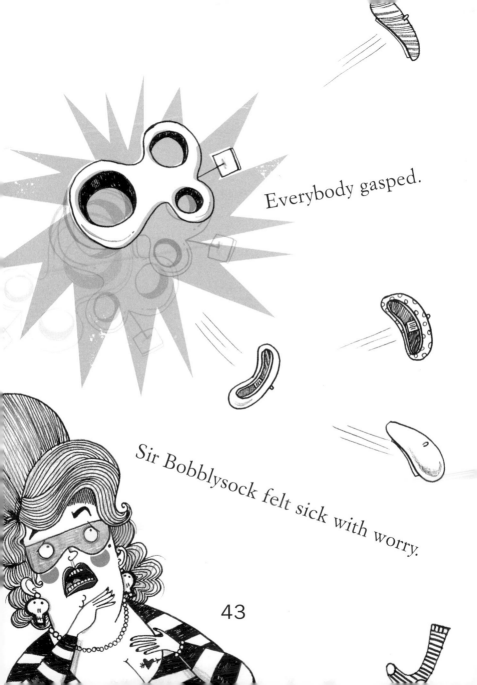

Everybody gasped.

Sir Bobblysock felt sick with worry.

43

But Claude saved the day!

Soon the Mayor arrived.
"Claude, you are a hero!" he cried.

He gave Claude a medal and
whisked him and Sir Bobblysock
off for a very nice dinner.

Back at Mr. and Mrs. Shinyshoes's house, Claude and Sir Bobblysock snuggled down in their bed. Claude closed his beady eyes.

A little later on, Mr. and Mrs. Shinyshoes came home from work.

"Where on earth did this medal come from?" asked Mrs. Shinyshoes. "Do you know anything about this, Claude?"

"Look, he's fast asleep!" said Mr. Shinyshoes. "We'll have to find out in the morning."

CHAPTER II

But the next morning, Mr. and Mrs. Shinyshoes had already left for work by the time Claude woke up.

He looked around for Sir Bobblysock, who often helped him put on his beret.

He would do this very importantly, as it was a very important job.

That morning, however, Sir
Bobblysock did not do his job
very importantly.

In fact, he didn't do it at all.
He just lay in bed like a sad, sick sock.

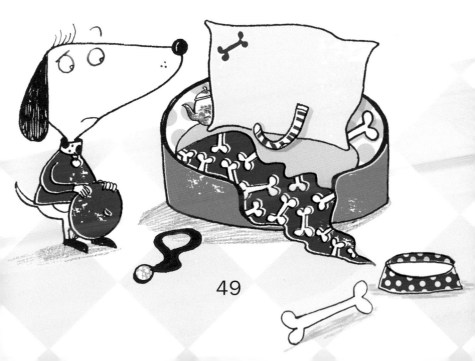

Claude looked at him very closely and frowned.

Sir Bobblysock did have the habit of sometimes pretending to be unwell.

He would lie there, all cross-eyed and floppy, waiting for Claude to find him and make a big fuss.

"Hmm...," said Claude, and he poked Sir Bobblysock in the tummy.

"Hmm...," he said again, and he prodded Sir Bobblysock's bobbles.

"Hmm...," he said for the third
time, and he took Sir Bobblysock's
temperature with a banana.

Claude thought for a minute.
"Sir Bobblysock," he said, "you are not very well. All that shopping and rushing around in the city has worn you out. I think I will have to take you to the hospital!"

So he did.

Claude didn't know where to
find an ambulance, so he
decided to make his own
instead.

He tucked Sir Bobblysock
safely under his arm and put
on his roller skates.

Shining his flashlight over his head
and shouting "Woo! Woo! Woo!"
for the siren, he skated to the
hospital, carrying Sir Bobblysock.

They arrived in no time at all.

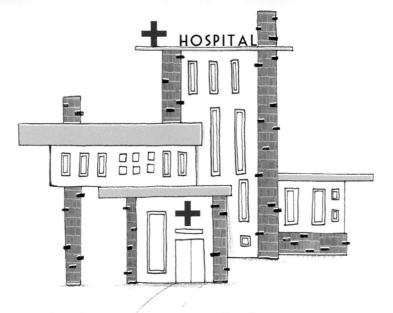

The hospital was a tall white
building that smelled of medicine
and sticky bandages.

Claude had only seen pictures of
hospitals in books. He thought that
a real one was much better, because
it wasn't flat and drawn on paper.

Claude popped Sir Bobblysock in a
wheelchair. They joined the end of
a long line of people, all waiting to
see the doctor.

DOCTOR

Claude didn't mind waiting,
because he had a tail to wag, but Sir
Bobblysock grumbled until Claude
got him a cup of milk and a cookie.

Eventually it was time for
Sir Bobblysock to see the doctor.
He was a tall, thin man with a tidy
moustache and something dangling
around his neck.

"I am Dr. Ivan Achinbum," he said.
"What seems to be the problem?"

Claude watched closely as
Dr. Achinbum prodded and poked
Sir Bobblysock's tummy, listened
to his heart with the dangly thing,
and took Sir Bobblysock's
temperature
(this time with
a thermometer,
not a banana).

Sir Bobblysock suddenly felt
very shy, so Claude explained.

"I see...," said Dr. Achinbum.
"Well, we will soon get you
feeling better again. Now let
me have a look at you."

Claude sniffed haughtily. He *always* found bananas were much better for taking temperatures.

Dr. Achinbum wrinkled his brow
and looked at Claude.

"I need to take your friend for an
X-ray so we can see what's going on
inside him. You stay here. We will
be back soon."

And he wheeled Sir Bobblysock out
of the room in his wheelchair.

Claude was now alone in the room.
At first he sat very still.

Then his eyes started to wander.
And then his paws.
And then his body.

He looked through all the drawers
and cupboards.

There were bandages and band-aids
and safety pins and lots of other
exciting things as well.

Last of all, he opened a tall
cupboard and gasped.

He gasped like this: *gasp!*

There, hanging all alone, was a
white coat exactly like the ones
Dr. Achinbum and the other
doctors were wearing.

Claude reached in, took the coat
off the hanger, and put it on.

"I look just like a doctor!" he said
and he twirled around to see
himself from every side.

Just then the door burst open. A nurse rushed in, looking red-faced and bothered.

"Oh, Doctor!" she cried. "Thank goodness I've found you!"

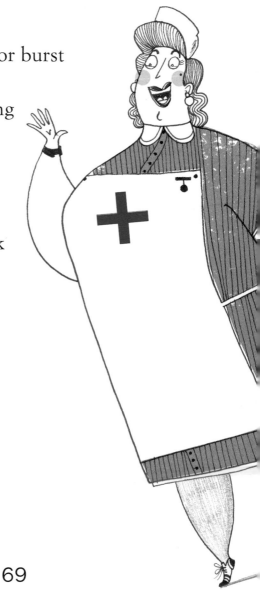

Claude looked around to find the doctor she was talking to, but there was no one else in the room.

She was talking to *him*!

"There's an emergency!" the nurse said, and with a deep breath she told him all about it.

Apparently, a group of wrestlers had come into the hospital, all complaining of a mystery illness, and now everyone in the waiting room had caught it!

The nurse said that Claude was the only doctor she could find. He would have to find out what this mysterious illness was.

Before Claude could explain that
he wasn't a real doctor—he was just
Claude—the nurse had hauled him
into the waiting room.

Well, everyone was in a terrible state.

The wrestlers were groaning in the corner. A large man covered in tattoos had dropped his embroidery and fainted by the potted plant. And some acrobats from the circus were lying on the front desk.

Claude had no idea what
to do! He tried to remember
when he had been unwell.

There was the time he had been
to an all-you-can-eat restaurant and
had eaten everything, including his
table.

He had been sick the next morning.
Maybe these people in the waiting
room had done the same.

76

But nobody smelled of noodles or
plywood, so that wasn't the problem.

Claude scratched his head.

Once, he had tried to knit a chair and ended up tying himself in knots, so he'd fallen over and bumped his head. He took a quick look around the waiting room.

No one had any knitting needles and nobody's head was bumpy.

No, that wasn't the problem.

Claude sighed. There was only one thing to do.

He rummaged around in his beret until he found an emergency banana and started to take people's temperatures with it.

But once he'd finished, he still didn't know what the problem was.

Nobody was too hot and
nobody was too cold.

THE GIGANTIC CLOCK
COMPANY

Claude was just wondering if he
should start prodding people,
when there came a noise from
behind the desk.

Bong! Bong! Bong! Bong! Bong!
Bong! Bong! Bong! Bong! Bong!
Bong!

It was the clock striking eleven.

Suddenly Claude felt himself starting to wobble! He felt like he was about to faint.

And it was exactly then that he realized what the mystery illness was.

"Nurse!" he cried, "I've solved the problem! These people have got eleven-o'clock-itis! What they need is a nice cup of tea and a sit-down. And possibly a cookie, if you have any?"

The nurse beamed a big smile,
spun around (Claude ducked),
and clattered off to the kitchen.

She came back carrying a huge tray
piled high with cups and cookies
and a gigantic teapot.

Claude helped her dish out the
drinks and cookies to the people
in the waiting room.

As soon as they had dunked their
cookies and slurped their tea, they
started to feel better.

It wasn't very long before the wrestlers
had each other in headlocks,

the acrobats were swinging from the light fixtures, and the man with the tattoos was busily fixing his embroidery.

Suddenly, Claude heard Dr. Achinbum talking to Sir Bobblysock.

He ran back to the office, took off the doctor's coat, and hung it up in the cupboard.

Then he quickly combed his ears
with a clipboard and sat down
neatly in the chair.

Seconds later, Dr. Achinbum
arrived, wheeling Sir Bobblysock—
who, Claude thought, looked
a lot better.

"He's all better!" said Dr. Achinbum to Claude. "We've solved the problem. He had a small hole in the heel, so we've had our best surgeon darn it and now he's as good as new!"

Claude was going to ask if Sir Bobblysock had behaved himself, but then he noticed that his friend was wearing a large sticker which said, "I was DARN good in the hospital," so he didn't bother.

"You are free to go home now!" said
Dr. Achinbum.

So Claude said thank you and
goodbye and set off with Sir
Bobblysock...

...but they didn't go by ambulance.

The wrestlers were so grateful to
Claude that they carried him and
Sir Bobblysock all the way home.

Claude and Sir Bobblysock decided
this was a very good way to travel.

Only perhaps not every day…

Keep your eyes open for Claude and Sir Bobblysock.
You never know where they'll turn up next.

CLAUDE.
at the Circus

An ordinary walk in the park leads to a walk on a tightrope when Claude accidentally joins the circus and becomes the star of the show!

$12.95 / 978-1-56145-702-1 / Fall 2013

CLAUDE.
at the Beach

A seaside holiday turns out to be more than Claude bargained for when he saves a swimmer, encounters pirates, and discovers treasure! *$12.95 / 978-1-56145-703-8 / Spring 2014*